No more kisses for Bernard!

Story & Pictures
by
Niki Daly

F
FRANCES LINCOLN
CHILDREN'S BOOKS

Everyone loved Bernard.

His aunts Lulu, Lola, Lilly and Tallulah
loved him to bits!

Whenever they visited, they covered
poor Bernard from head to toe with...

squeaky-sweet-
hello kisses

lip-sticky-red-and-glow kisses

sneaky-on-the-nose kisses

and smoochy-got-to-go kisses

It drove
Bernard
Bonkers!

After their visits, Mama had to wash
a mess of kisses off Bernard's face.
"Maybe a hello and goodbye kiss is all
you really need," said Mama.

But Bernard said,

"No more kisses!"

And he meant it!

On his birthday when his kissy-kissy aunts arrived,
Bernard was prepared!
"Happy Birthday!" they sang, and gave him his presents.
Then they lined up for their 'Thank-you-very-much-
for-my-lovely-birthday-present kiss'.
Instead, Bernard thanked them politely…
then he quickly pulled down his visor.

And before you could say "kissy-kissy"
Aunt Tallulah swung open his visor and stuck
a fat, smudgy one right on his nose!

That did it!

"No kisses!"

wailed Bernard,
bursting into tears.

"When someone says *no*, they mean *no*,"
Aunt Lulu scolded Aunt Tallulah.
"Children need to be respected," said Aunt Lola.
"You're always breaking rules, Tallulah," said Aunt Lilly.

"I know. I'm sorry, Bernard. May I have a little huggles?" said Aunt Tallulah.

"No hugs!" wailed Bernard, frowning. And he meant it!

Woof!

The aunts looked too sad for words.
They loved him more than all the hugs,
kisses and birthday wishes in the world.
"I love you more than words can say,"
said Aunt Tallulah, blowing Bernard a kiss.

"No kisses!"

yelled Bernard, ducking out of the way.

"How about a paper kiss then?" asked Aunt Tallulah.

"What's a paper kiss?" asked Bernard.

"Give me a piece of paper and I'll show you," said Aunt Tallulah.

Bernard gave Aunt Tallulah a page from his rainbow pad. He watched Aunt Tallulah take out her lipstick and draw six red kisses on the pink paper.

Then, using Bernard's scissors, she cut hearts around the kisses.

"There!" said Aunt Tallulah. "With all my love and a kiss for each of your birthdays."

Bernard loved his paper kisses.

Now everyone wanted to cut out frilly paper hearts
and draw kisses for the birthday boy.
Bernard shared his rainbow paper, felt tip pens,
glitter glues and his fancy scissors.

At the end of the party there were more than enough paper hearts and kisses for everyone.

But…

By the time the aunts left, Bernard was covered
from head to toe in bits of rainbow pad,
glitter glue and felt tip markers.

So Mama gave him a bath.

And when he was squeaky clean
and ready for bed, she said,
"Now, how about a special kiss
for your Mama?"

Bernard thought for a while...

and then he gave his Mama **and** Papa

a nice-and-simple
peck-on-the-dimple,

good night-sleep tight
Bernard kiss!

Little Baa

Kim Lewis

WALKER BOOKS

AND SUBSIDIARIES

LONDON • BOSTON • SYDNEY

Little Baa frisked in the field.
His Ma ate quietly beside him.

Spring and bounce and skip went Baa,
running through the grass with his friends.

Little Baa ran along the fence,
hopping over rocks.
Spring and bounce and skip
went Baa.

Soon he left his friends behind.

Then Little Baa
grew tired. He found
a hollow near some
trees and settled
down for a nap.

Ma ate grass until little by little
she was far along the field.

When Ma finished eating, she looked around.
"Where's my Little Baa?" she said.

She couldn't see his spotty ears.
She couldn't smell his familiar smell.

She couldn't hear his little baa.
"Baa!" she called. "Where's my Little Baa?"

"Maa!" called lots of little lambs.
They came towards her, one by one.

"You're not mine," sniffed Ma to each.

None of them were her very own
the way Little Baa was hers.

The little lambs ran to their mothers.
Ma sniffed among the ewes.

"Have you got my Little Baa?" asked Ma.

"Go away," said the ewes, and stamped their feet.
"These lambs are ours, not yours."

Ma trotted sadly on.

The sun was starting to go down.

Ma's voice became a lonely sound.

She couldn't rest or eat or think.

"Baa!" she cried. "Please answer me!"

But there was only silence in the field.

Then the shepherd came with his collie, Floss.
He heard Ma calling and saw she was alone.
"Where's your little lamb?" he said to Ma
and strode off through the grass.

Little Baa woke up feeling cold and hungry.
He stretched and blinked and then he saw
the beady eyes of a border collie.

Floss didn't have Ma's spotty ears.
Floss didn't have his mother's smell.
Worst of all, Floss went "Bark!"
"You're not my Ma!" said Little Baa.

"Ma!" cried Little Baa, running every which way.

"Maa!" cried Little Baa, running round in circles.

"Wait, Floss," said the shepherd softly.

From far across the field,

Ma picked out the little sound.

It was the sound she wanted most of all

in the whole wide new spring world.

First Ma walked. Then she trotted.

Soon she was running fast.

"Baa!" she called. "Baa, Baa, Baaa!"

Little Baa ran to Ma.

He ran and ran and ran.

"Ma!" he said. "Ma, Maa, Maaa!"

Ma sniffed Little Baa all over, baaing gently.

"Where were you, Ma?" asked Little Baa.

"Looking everywhere for you," she said.

Ma stood quietly while he fed
because Little Baa was oh so hungry.
Then Little Baa snuggled down with Ma.

"Ma?" said Little Baa sleepily.
"Are you still there?"
"I am, Little Baa, I'm here," said Ma,
lying quietly beside him.